ONE CITY, TWO BROTHERS

Barefoot Books
2067 Massachusetts Ave
Cambridge, MA 02140

Text copyright © 2007 by Chris Smith
Illustrations copyright © 2007 by Aurélia Fronty
The moral right of Chris Smith to be identified as the author
and Aurélia Fronty to be identified as the illustrator of this work has been asserted

This book has been printed on 100% acid-free paper
Graphic design by Judy Linard, London. Color separation by Grafiscan, Verona
Printed and bound in China by Printplus Ltd

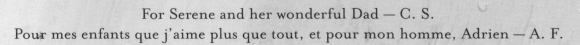

This book was typeset in Mrs Eaves 15 on 26 point and Trajon and Lithos Regular
The illustrations were prepared in acrylics

Library of Congress Cataloging-in-Publication Data

Smith, Chris, 1947-
    One city, two brothers : the story of Jerusalem / Chris Smith ; [illustrated by] Aurélia Fronty.
      p. cm.
    Summary: To settle an inheritance dispute between two brothers, King Solomon tells a tale
of how Jerusalem came to be founded.
    ISBN-13: 978-1-84686-042-3 (hardcover : alk. paper)
    [1. Folklore--Middle East. 2. Jerusalem--Folklore.]   I. Fronty, Aurélia, ill. II. Title.
    PZ8.1.S6482One 2007
    398.20933--dc22

2006023463

3 5 7 9 8 6 4 2

ONE CITY, TWO BROTHERS

Written by *Chris Smith*

Illustrated by *Aurélia Fronty*

Barefoot Books
Celebrating Art and Story

Once, wise King Solomon* ruled in the city of Jerusalem. He built a magnificent temple in the city, a special and sacred place for his people. Every day, the king sat in his palace receiving visitors, offering guidance to those who asked, and judgement for those who broke his laws.

One day, two brothers stood before the king. Their father had died recently, and they were arguing about who should inherit the family land. They came to the king for advice.

"By law, it should be mine!" said one.

"It's only fair that I have my share!" shouted the other.

The wise king listened to them argue for a while. They grew louder and angrier until finally he held up his hand for silence.

"Let me tell you a story," he said, "from long ago, before there was a city here, before any temple had been built on this land."

This is the story that Solomon* told.

Long ago, a river valley curved and curled its way through the land from the hills in the east to the sea in the west, its steep sides lined with orchards of olives and almonds. Near the head of the valley, where the river curled around the foot of a rocky hill, there were two villages, each a cluster of white stone huts and animal pens. Two brothers farmed a piece of land on the flat valley floor between the two villages, where the soil was rich and deep — perfect for farming.

The elder brother lived in a village on the valley side, above the field they shared. The younger lived in the other village, a little down the valley, below the field. Two paths linked the villages — one over the hill that separated them, and the other along the valley floor past their field.

Every autumn, after the first rains, each brother brought his donkey, and together they plowed the earth and sowed the grain. Every winter, the grain sprouted and grew until springtime, when the heads of wheat swelled and ripened, turning gold by early summer. Then the brothers brought their scythes, cutting and threshing the wheat, and pouring the grain into sacks.

When all the work was done, the brothers counted up the sacks of grain, dividing them equally, half and half. Each kept an equal portion of straw for his animals' bedding and wheat to grind into flour for baking bread.

Then autumn came around and it was time to start plowing again. In this way, the years passed.

The elder brother married and soon had a handful of children
to feed at home. Happily, his share of the harvest always gave
him enough to last the winter. He was content. The younger
brother never married. Some say he never found the right woman;
others say he liked the quiet life. Whatever the truth, he too was
content with his lot.

One summer, the harvest was the best ever. Each brother stacked
the heavy bags of grain: twenty bags each. The elder brother had
just finished when he thought of his younger brother.

"I'm so lucky to have a family," he thought. "When I'm old, they will be there to take care of me. But my poor brother has nobody. He'll need to save for his old age. He needs this grain more than I do."

He decided to give his younger brother a surprise gift. When it was dark, he loaded three sacks of grain onto his donkey and led it up over the hill behind his house and down to his brother's village on the other side. It was a cloudy night, without moon or stars to light the path, but he knew the route so well he could have found his way with his eyes closed. Very quietly, he tiptoed into the store and added the three sacks to his brother's pile. He walked home smiling at the thought of his brother's face in the morning.

The next day, over breakfast, his wife asked him about the harvest.

"Only seventeen sacks this year," he said, "but that will be enough if we are careful."

His wife looked puzzled. "Why only seventeen? It looked like a good crop."

Her husband just shrugged and smiled.

While the family was finishing breakfast, his wife ducked into the store, returning a few moments later.

"Husband, are you so tired you have forgotten how to count?"

"What do you mean?" he asked.

"I've been in the store and there are twenty sacks, not seventeen."

"That's impossible!"

But, when he went to the store, he saw that it was true. Twenty sacks of grain!

"How can that be?" he wondered. "I must have been dreaming."

That evening, after sunset, he took another three sacks of grain to his brother's store. This time, to rest his donkey, he took the easier path along the valley floor. Next morning, over breakfast, he explained to his wife that there would only be seventeen sacks after all, as he had given three away.

He pressed his finger to his lips. "It's a secret," he whispered.

His wife looked at him suspiciously. "Are you sure?" she asked.

"I'm quite sure. Come, I'll show you."

But when they looked in the store there were still twenty sacks. His wife was not pleased.

"Why are you teasing me like this?" she demanded. "You should tell me the truth."

"Could it be a miracle?" he wondered. "Or am I just getting old and forgetful?"

On the third night, he set off at sunset with another three sacks, determined to give his gift.

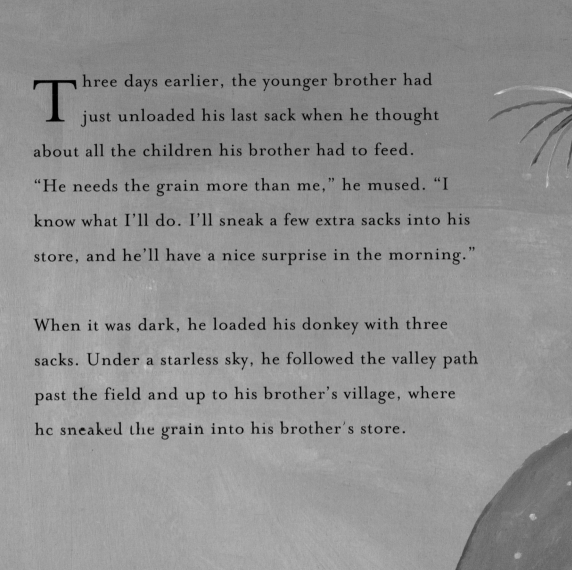

Three days earlier, the younger brother had just unloaded his last sack when he thought about all the children his brother had to feed. "He needs the grain more than me," he mused. "I know what I'll do. I'll sneak a few extra sacks into his store, and he'll have a nice surprise in the morning."

When it was dark, he loaded his donkey with three sacks. Under a starless sky, he followed the valley path past the field and up to his brother's village, where he sneaked the grain into his brother's store.

The next day, the younger brother noticed that something was odd. There were too many sacks of grain in his store. He counted them — twenty new sacks. He'd given away three, so there should only be seventeen left. How could there be twenty? Could it have been a dream?

All day he was puzzled, and when night fell he loaded three more sacks onto his donkey, determined to help his brother. This time, he took the shorter path over the hill, unloaded three more sacks into his brother's store and crept back home.

Next morning, he checked his grain store again, and there were still twenty sacks. "How can that be? I must be imagining things," he thought. "But tonight I really will do it."

That evening, for the third time, he set out up the hill for his brother's village. This time, the moon was full and the night was clear. As he reached the top of the hill, he saw his brother walking toward him leading a donkey. It was as if he were walking toward his own reflection.

Without even speaking, each understood the reason for his brother's journey. Their hearts filled with happiness as they realized the love they had both been shown. That hill, between the two villages, was the place where the city of Jerusalem began. That blessed spot, where the two brothers met, became the site of the holy temple.

With these words, Solomon* finished his story. The two men stood in silence, and everyone in the court waited to see what they would say. After a long time, the older man looked up.

"Brother," he said. "What was once our father's is now ours. Not yours, not mine, but ours to share."

The brothers embraced and left the court side by side. From that time on, they and their families lived happily together. And there was no story their children enjoyed listening to more than the story of the two brothers, first told by wise King Solomon*.

JERUSALEM

If you ever happen to be traveling, and come to the point where Europe meets Asia, and where Asia meets Africa, you will find a city bursting with history and mystery. Enter the city walls, explore the tangle of alleyways and markets, and you will discover ancient places of worship at every turn. There is a magnificent mosque with a vast golden dome; a labyrinth of churches and chapels; and a huge holy wall where thousands pray daily.

Every year, as far back as can be remembered, pilgrims have traveled to the city from all over the world to pray and worship. Its name? The Arabs call it *Al-Quds*, the holy city; in Hebrew it is *Yerushalaym*; in English it is Jerusalem.

How did such a city come to be? This story gives an answer. The tale can be heard in synagogues around the world, told as a Jewish fable. It is also shared by Palestinian Arabs living in and around the city,

told as an Arab folk tale. The story was first written down some two hundred years ago by a traveler to Jerusalem, who had heard it from a local Arab farmer. Since then, it has moved between people and places throughout the world. It is not part of the holy books of Jews, Muslims or Christians; rather, it is a simple folk tale, passed from storyteller to storyteller for hundreds, perhaps thousands, of years, kept alive by the power of its message.

Jerusalem has remained a holy city, with a special place in the stories and faith of Jews, Christians and Muslims. Jerusalem is the place where Abraham* lived and worshipped, and where his sons, Isaac* and Ishmael*, were born. Both Jews and Arabs are said to be descended from Abraham* through these two sons. Jerusalem is the city where King David* ruled, after defeating Goliath with his slingshot. Soon after this, Solomon* came to the throne, building the temple, which was later destroyed by invaders.

Later, Jerusalem became the city where Jesus* taught. Later still, it became the place from which the Prophet Mohammed* made his sacred journey to heaven to receive God's message, and where two magnificent mosques were built on the site of the old temple.

Since then, Jerusalem has seen many wars and many rulers. Arabs, Turks and Europeans have all had their turn. Today, the city is still bitterly disputed, claimed by both Israelis and Palestinians. Nobody knows if, one day, there will be peace. Perhaps, if Solomon* were alive today, he might tell this story to help point the way.

*In the Muslim tradition, the words "may peace be upon him" are traditionally spoken out of respect after mentioning the name of a prophet. The asterisk in the text is placed there to invite the Muslim reader to add this blessing to the reading, if desired.

Barefoot Books
Celebrating Art and Story

At Barefoot Books, we celebrate art and story that opens
the hearts and minds of children from all walks of life, inspiring
them to read deeper, search further, and explore their own creative gifts.
Taking our inspiration from many different cultures, we focus on themes that
encourage independence of spirit, enthusiasm for learning, and sharing of
the world's diversity. Interactive, playful and beautiful, our products
combine the best of the present with the best of the past to
educate our children as the caretakers of tomorrow.

Live Barefoot!
Join us at *www.barefootbooks.com*